Duck and Hippo
THE SECRET VALENTINE

By **JONATHAN LONDON**   Illustrated by **ANDREW JOYNER**

two lions

Published by Two Lions, New York

www.apub.com

Amazon, the Amazon logo, and Two Lions are trademarks of Amazon.com, Inc., or its affiliates.

ISBN-13: 9781503900356
ISBN-10: 1503900355

The illustrations are rendered in brush
and ink with wash and pencil and then digitally colored.
Series design by Abby Dening
Book design by AndWorld Design

Printed and bound in the United States
First Edition
3 5 7 9 10 8 6 4 2

For sweet Maureen, Aaron, and Sean & Steph
—J. L.

For my beloved Beck
—A. J.

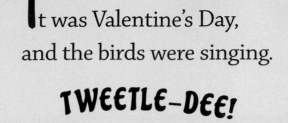

It was Valentine's Day,
and the birds were singing.

TWEETLE-DEE!

But Duck thought, **WAIT!**
I DON'T have a valentine!

Then—*tweetle-dee!*—
I have an idea!

Later that day, while Hippo was busy dusting . . .

KNOCK! KNOCK! KNOCK!

Who could it be? wondered Hippo.
I know! It must be Duck!
At least, I **HOPE** *it's Duck!*

But when Hippo opened the door . . .

. . . no one was there!

Then he saw a card
and picked it up.
There was a red rose on it
above a big red heart.

Hippo opened the card and read:

HAPPY
VALENTINE'S
DAY!
Come to the Park
Today at 4pm

And bring
something for
your Valentine!

But there was no
name on the card.

Hippo looked all around,
hoping to catch a glimpse
of his valentine.

"DUCK! DUCK!" he called.
"Are you *there*?"

But all he saw was a white feather

floating down,

landing softly

on the ground.

Meanwhile, Turtle was snoozing beside the pond, dreaming about his valentine. Suddenly he heard a tiny splash.

SPLOOP!

He woke up . . .
and almost rolled into the water!

"Yipes!"

And there, on a lily pad, was a card
with a big red heart on it.

The heart reminded him, just a little bit,
of a pizza with a slice out of it!

But there was no name on the card.

Turtle looked all around,
hoping to catch a glimpse of his valentine.
"PIG! Are you *there*?"

But all he saw were some birds.

TWEETLE-DEE!

HAPPY VALENTINE'S DAY!
Come to the Park
Today at 4pm
And bring
Something for
your Valentine!

Later, Pig was all alone,
tossing pizza dough at Pig's Pizza,
when she heard the bell above the door.

RING-A-DING
DING!

She looked . . .
and the flying pizza
landed on her head!

SPLAT!

HAPPY
VALENTINE'S
DAY!
Come to the Park
Today at 4pm

And bring
something for
your Valentine!

Then she saw a card with a big red
heart on it under the door.

But there was no name on the card.

Pig blushed and raced outside,
hoping to catch a glimpse of her valentine.
"TURTLE! Are you *there*?"

HUSHA-SHUSHA-SHUSHA!

But all she saw was
the street sweeper.

ELEPHANT'S MARKET

Meanwhile, Elephant was checking
his mailbox, hoping to find a
Valentine's Day card . . .

and he did!

"*HO!*" boomed Elephant.

HAPPY
VALENTINE'S
DAY!
Come to the Park
Today at 4pm
And bring
Something for
your Valentine!

But there was no name on the card.

He spun on one leg,
trying to catch a glimpse of his valentine.

"DUCK! PIG!
Are you *there*?"

He got so dizzy
that he fell on his trunk.

SMACK!

He sat up and rubbed it.
Then he held the card
against his heart and beamed.

Back at Hippo's house, the clock was ticking.

TICK-TOCK!
TICK-TOCK!

BRUSH-BRUSHA-
BRUSHA!

It was only one o'clock.
Hippo brushed his teeth.

He put on his favorite bow tie and looked in the mirror.

Then he smiled so wide that his tie popped off.

BOP!

At two o'clock, Turtle went outside and looked at himself in the pond. A fish looked back. It seemed to be blowing kisses at him!

SMOOCH!

SMOOCH!

SMOOOOOOCH!

Then slowly, slowly, Turtle started walking,
holding a basket filled with doughnuts.

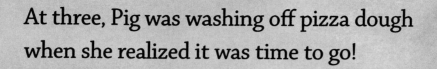

At three, Pig was washing off pizza dough when she realized it was time to go!

SCRUBBA-DUBBA-
DUBBA!

She put on her favorite blue dress and sang, *"I'm in love! I'm in love! I'm in love!"*

Then she put her favorite pizza in a box and taped a Valentine's Day card to the lid.

At three thirty, Elephant wrapped his sore trunk around a batch of flowers and anxiously marched toward the park.

At fifteen minutes to four,
Hippo *rushed* toward the park,
with a box of chocolates and flowers,
hoping that Duck would be there.

And at four o'clock . . .

everybody showed up at the park
at the *exact same time!*

But . . .

. . . where, OH WHERE, was Duck?

Suddenly, Duck leaped out of a bush, danced all around, and said,
"TA–DA! *I'm* the secret valentine!"

Then she gave Hippo a rose,
winked, and said,
"The *best* valentines are *friends*!"

"HURRAY!" everyone cheered.

And they all passed around cards,
and chocolates and flowers,
and doughnuts,
and Pig's favorite pizza,
and yelled,

"THE *BEST* VALENTINES ARE *FRIENDS*!
HAPPY VALENTINE'S DAY!"